P9-APY-091

Don't Bake
That Snake!

Read other

SPENCER'S adventures

SPENCER'S adventures

Don't Bake That Snake!

by

Gary Hogg

illustrated by Chuck Slack

A
LITTLE APPLE
PAPERBACK

SCHOLASTIC INC.
New York   Toronto   London   Auckland   Sydney

For my parents, who taught me to laugh, learn, and love.

If you purchased this book without a cover, you should be aware that this book is stolen property. It was reported as "unsold and destroyed" to the publisher, and neither the author nor the publisher has received any payment for this "stripped book."

No part of this publication may be reproduced in whole or in part, or stored in a retrieval system, or transmitted in any form or by any means, electronic, mechanical, photocopying, recording, or otherwise, without written permission of the publisher. For information regarding permission, write to Scholastic Inc., 555 Broadway, New York, NY 10012.

ISBN 0-590-93939-4

Text copyright © 1997 by Gary Hogg.
Illustrations copyright © 1996 by Scholastic Inc.
All rights reserved. Published by Scholastic Inc.
LITTLE APPLE PAPERBACKS is a trademark and/or registered trademark of Scholastic Inc.

12 11 10 9 8 7 6 5 4 3 2 1   7 8 9/9 0 1/0 2/0

Printed in the U.S.A.   40
First Scholastic printing, October 1997

CONTENTS

Chapter One

Egg War

"This better be good," said Spencer as he led his best friend, Josh Porter, into the kitchen.

"Don't worry," replied Josh. "It'll knock your socks off." Josh reached into his backpack and pulled out a brown paper bag.

"I hope it's a python," said Spencer. "You know I love snakes." He peeked into the bag and then punched Josh in the arm. "You call this a big deal? It's just flour. We've got lots of flour."

"Oh, yeah?" said Josh. "Does your flour set up as hard as concrete? This is plaster. It's the stuff they use to make casts for broken arms and legs."

"Excellent!" said Spencer. "We can be doctors. All we need is something broken that we can put a cast on."

"That's easy," replied Josh. "Let's just bust something."

"Dr. Porter, I like the way you think," said Spencer. He started looking around the kitchen for something to break.

"How about the toaster?" asked Josh. "I've broken our toaster twice. I'm good at it."

"We can't put a cast on the toaster," said Spencer. "My mom would notice right away."

Josh opened the refrigerator and stuck

his head in. "Wow, talk about leftovers." He lifted the lid of a blue bowl and looked in. "Gross! This stuff looks like lizard brains."

"That's leftover Looney Tuna Surprise," said Spencer. "Believe me, lizard brains couldn't taste any worse than that junk."

Josh started to shut the refrigerator door when he spotted a row of eggs. He picked up one of the eggs and gently tossed it to Spencer. Spencer threw the egg back to Josh. Soon the boys were having a fast game of egg toss.

Higher and higher the egg soared. And then it happened. The egg crashed into the ceiling. Spencer and Josh looked up at the slimy yolk clinging to the ceiling above their heads.

"Now look what you did!" said Spencer.

"I didn't do that," insisted Josh. "You did!"

"Oh, yeah?" said Spencer, picking up another egg. "Take this, Mr. Egghead." He reared back and let the egg fly. Josh ducked and the egg smashed into the wall.

Josh quickly grabbed an egg and launched it straight at Spencer's head. The egg missed Spencer and kept flying. Just then, Spencer's sister, Amber, walked around the corner. The egg splattered right on the front of her brand-new shirt.

Amber just stood there. Her eyes crossed as she looked down at the yolk clinging to her clothes.

"It must have knocked her goofy," said Josh.

Suddenly Amber opened her mouth. The scream that came out was so loud and so horrible, the windows started to

rattle and dogs all over the neighbor-
hood began to bark.

The boys were about to make a run
for it when Mrs. Burton came rushing
into the room.

Chapter Two

Garbage Face

"What on earth is going on?" demanded Mrs. Burton.

Amber pointed at the boys and yelled, "Those creeps egged me."

Mrs. Burton examined the egg on Amber's shirt and said to the boys, "I want an explanation for this and I want it this second."

"It was an accident," blurted out Spencer. "I was just showing Josh our eggs when I dropped one. For some strange reason, it bounced off the floor and smacked Amber."

"The egg bounced?" asked Mrs. Burton. At that instant, the egg that was stuck to the ceiling came loose. It landed right on Mrs. Burton's head.

"Oops," said Josh.

Spencer's mother closed her eyes and bit her lip. When she opened her eyes, she said, "Let me guess. I have egg slime in my hair."

"Just a little," said Spencer.

"He's lying!" shouted Amber. "There's egg goo all over your hair. It looks like a giant bird had an accident on your head."

"Okay, Amber," said Mrs. Burton. "Go clean up while I deal with these two." Amber stuck her tongue out at the boys and stormed out of the kitchen.

Mrs. Burton put her hands on her hips

and said, "You boys have broken some pretty big rules here."

"We broke some pretty big eggs too," added Josh.

"I want you to clean up this mess, and I mean every last drop of slime," said Mrs. Burton. "Then, Josh, you go home, and Spencer, you go to your room for a time-out. Have I made myself clear?"

"Yes, Mom," said Spencer. "But there's something you need to know."

"What?" asked Mrs. Burton.

"You have a piece of eggshell stuck on the end of your nose," said Spencer.

Mrs. Burton snatched the shell off her nose and marched out of the room.

"Don't worry, Josh," said Spencer. "I have a secret weapon when it comes to cleaning." He walked over to the hall closet and pulled out the vacuum cleaner. "Josh, meet Garbage Face."

"I don't think you're supposed to suck

up egg guts with a vacuum, even if its name is Garbage Face," said Josh.

"Eggs are no problem for this guy," said Spencer. "One time, I got in a food fight with Amber. There were beans and junk all over the place. Garbage Face ate every last drop and then let out a little burp."

"Do you think Garbage Face could swallow a person?" asked Josh. "I wouldn't mind vacuuming up my big sister."

"I already tried it on Amber," answered Spencer. "I guess some things are too gross even for Garbage Face."

It took Spencer, Josh, and Garbage Face just a few minutes to clean up the remains of the egg war.

Josh was in such a hurry to leave, he forgot about his bag of plaster. Spencer put Garbage Face away and headed for his room. It was time for a time-out.

Chapter Three

The Deal with Appeal

A time-out really wasn't much of a punishment for Spencer. He'd had so many of them in his life, they didn't bother him at all. Of course, he didn't let his parents in on that little secret.

Eventually the bedroom door opened and Mrs. Burton stuck her head in. "Spencer, your time-out is over. I hope you learned your lesson."

"I sure did," Spencer said. "No more

scrambled eggs on the ceiling."

"Good," said Mrs. Burton. "Now come to dinner." She didn't have to tell Spencer twice. He was hungry.

Spencer rushed into the kitchen and plopped down in his chair. "What are we eating?" he asked.

"We're finishing off the last of the Looney Tuna Surprise," Mrs. Burton said.

"Gag," moaned Spencer. "Mom, don't you know the *surprise* is when you're still alive after eating the Looney Tuna Surprise?"

"Very funny, young man," said Mrs. Burton. "Josh left a bag of flour on the counter. As soon as you're done eating, I want you to bring it back to him."

Spencer ate a few bites of his dinner and smushed the rest around his plate. Picking up the bag of plaster, he headed out. "I'll be back soon," he called out as he shut the back door.

Running down the sidewalk, Spencer spotted a bike coming fast and heading straight at him. Spencer jumped off the sidewalk just as the bike zoomed past and crashed into a tree.

"Oh, no!" yelled Spencer, and ran over to the accident. Sitting in the grass, rubbing his head, was the biggest kid in sixth grade, Big Jim McNalley.

"Are you all right?" asked Spencer.

"I hope not," answered Big Jim. "That's my third crash today. I'm trying to break my leg."

"Do you think you busted it this time?" asked Spencer.

"Doesn't feel like it," said Big Jim sadly.

"Too bad," said Spencer. "Why do you want a broken leg?"

"I want a cast," said Big Jim. "Ned Bailey got one and was instantly popular. All the girls wanted to sign his cast."

Spencer looked at the bag of plaster and then at Big Jim. "You don't have to break your leg," he said. "I'll sell you a cast."

"What are you talking about?" asked Big Jim.

"This bag is full of plaster," said Spencer. "You could use it to make your own cast."

Big Jim looked in the bag to make sure Spencer was telling the truth. "How much do you want for it?" he asked.

Spencer thought for a second. Anyone dumb enough to crash his bike into a tree on purpose would probably pay plenty. "Fifty bucks," said Spencer.

"You're crazy," said Big Jim. "I wouldn't give you more than two dollars."

"Sold!" yelled Spencer. "You just bought yourself a cast."

"Great," said Big Jim. "Give me the plaster and I'll give you the money later."

Spencer sighed. He knew it was too good to be true. Besides being the biggest kid in sixth grade, Big Jim told the biggest lies. Spencer was pretty sure he would never see a cent of the money. He gripped the bag tight and started off for Josh's house.

"Wait a minute," said Big Jim, jumping up. "I'm not lying. I swear you'll get your dough."

"No deal," said Spencer firmly.

"I'll prove it to you," said Big Jim. "You can keep something of mine until I get you the cash."

"You don't have anything I want," said Spencer.

"I've got a really cool snake," said Big Jim.

Spencer stopped dead in his tracks. He loved snakes. Suddenly this was the deal with appeal.

"He's right here in my backpack," said Big Jim. He reached into his pack and pulled out a snake. It was a foot long and bright green.

"His name is Stretch and he's very valuable," said Big Jim. "Remember, I'm just letting you borrow him. If anything happens to this snake, I'll make sure something happens to you."

"I'll take really good care of him," said Spencer, taking hold of the snake. Stretch curled around Spencer's arm and stuck out his forked tongue.

Big Jim put the bag of plaster in his backpack. He climbed onto his bike and took off like a flash. Big Jim had a big cast to make.

Spencer and Stretch headed for home. Spencer had plans for his new fork-tongued friend. He'd wait until tomor-row to explain to Josh where the plaster went.

Chapter Four

Knock-knock

When Spencer got home, he headed straight for Amber's room. Marching up to the closed door, he called out, "Knock-knock."

"Go away," shouted Amber, "or I'll knock-knock you out."

"Knock-knock," repeated Spencer.

"I'm not going to answer you," yelled Amber.

"Knock-knock," said Spencer.

"Don't you understand? I'm not interested in your stupid joke," said Amber.

"Knock-knock," said Spencer again.

"Okay, if it will make you go away I'll play along, but this better be good," said Amber. "Who's there?"

"Justa," said Spencer.

"Justa who?" asked Amber, opening the door.

"Justa snake," yelled Spencer, waving Stretch in front of Amber's face. Spencer's sister didn't scream like he thought she would. She didn't faint. She didn't even slam the door. She said, "Oh, he's so cute," and reached out and took Stretch from Spencer.

"Hey, since when did you start liking snakes?" asked Spencer.

"Since I needed one for evidence that you're breaking the rules," answered Amber. With that, she headed down the hall.

Spencer chased after his sister. "Amber, please don't tell on me. That snake is worth two bucks. I'll split the money with you if you don't tattle."

Amber stopped and shoved Stretch at Spencer. "If I don't have the money by tomorrow night, I'm turning you in."

"Don't worry," said Spencer, taking hold of the snake.

Spencer took Stretch and went straight to his bedroom. He couldn't take the chance of being caught with a snake. He used to have a pet snake named Junior. For some reason, this snake had a crush on his mother. However, it was a one-sided love affair.

When Mrs. Burton found Junior in her purse making goo-goo eyes at her, she screamed so loud Junior almost jumped out of his skin.

The time she discovered Junior in her sock drawer, forming the shape of a heart with his body, she was so upset she didn't wear socks for a week.

Junior was sent to a pet store and Spencer was warned never to bring anything that slithers into the Burtons' house again.

Spencer and Stretch stayed in Spencer's bedroom for the rest of the night. They had a wonderful slumber party. Spencer told Stretch his best scary stories. But Spencer knew that none of his stories came close to the weird things Stretch had seen living with Big Jim.

The next morning, Spencer woke up early. He got dressed quickly and wolfed down his breakfast. He couldn't wait to get to school and introduce Stretch to Josh.

Chapter Five

Stretching the Truth

Spencer found Josh waiting for him at the edge of the playground.

"I left my bag of plaster at your house," said Josh. "I hope you brought it with you."

"I brought something a lot better than plaster," said Spencer. "I've got a snake."

"A real one or a rubber one?" asked Josh.

"Does this guy look like he's made out

of rubber?" asked Spencer, pulling the snake out of his backpack. "His name is Stretch."

"Awesome," said Josh.

"He's not really mine," said Spencer. "I'm just keeping him until Big Jim McNalley pays me the money he owes me for your plaster."

"You sold my plaster?" asked Josh.

"I couldn't pass up the deal," said Spencer. "He's paying two dollars for it. I have to give Amber a buck to keep quiet about the snake, but that leaves us a whole dollar to split."

"You dummy," said Josh. "I paid three dollars for that plaster."

"Oops," said Spencer. "Well, at least we get to play with this great snake. It will be fun, but we can't lose him. Big Jim will flatten me if anything happens to Stretch."

Suddenly Stretch started to squirm

and wiggle wildly. He was like a wet noodle that had come to life. He squeezed free from Spencer's grip and hit the ground. The snake quickly disappeared into a pile of leaves.

"Get that snake!" yelled Spencer, diving into the leaves.

Spencer and Josh were so busy with the snake hunt, they didn't even notice Big Jim come walking up.

"Hey, how do you guys like my new cast?" asked Big Jim.

Spencer and Josh stared. A big, weird-looking cast covered Big Jim's right foot.

"It would have looked better if you'd taken off your shoe before putting on the cast," said Spencer.

"I didn't think of that," said Big Jim. "What are you guys looking for?"

"We're, uh, looking for a pencil," replied Spencer.

"Let me help you look," said Big Jim,

bending over and looking in the leaves.

"No!" screamed Spencer. "We'll find it. You'd better go. I'll bet there are a lot of girls waiting to sign your cast."

"You're right," said Big Jim. "I'm bringing the money I owe you to the school carnival tonight. You'd better have Stretch and he'd better be just the way he was when you took him."

Spencer swallowed hard. "Don't worry, I'm looking for — I mean, looking after Stretch all the time."

"Good," said Big Jim, heading to class.

The boys left no leaf unturned in their search for Stretch. But they couldn't find a trace of that snake.

"He's a goner." Josh sighed.

"Don't even think that," insisted Spencer.

"Well, I don't see him," replied Josh, "and school's about to start. I don't know about you, but I'm heading in.

Miss Bingham said that if I had any more tardies, she would call my mom."

Josh picked up his pack and headed for school. Spencer poked around in the leaves for Stretch one last time, but he knew Josh was right. Stretch had hit the road.

Chapter Six

Cakewalk

Spencer walked slowly into school. He sat down at his desk and looked at his teacher, Miss Bingham. Nobody loved school as much as Miss Bingham. She always looked happy.

"Students, you know that the school carnival is tonight," she said. "Our class has been put in charge of one of the booths."

T.J.'s hand shot into the air. "Is it the

spook alley?" he asked. "I have some great ideas that will gross everybody out."

"No, our booth is going to be much more fun than a spook alley," replied Miss Bingham. "We're in charge of the cakewalk."

"Cakewalk," moaned T.J. "You can't gross anyone out with a cake."

"Oh, yeah?" said Rex. "You've never tasted my mom's fruitcake."

"Before you get all worked up, let me explain what a cakewalk is," said Miss Bingham. "A cakewalk is just like musical chairs. But instead of using chairs, the people walk from number to number. Every time the music stops, the person who isn't on a number must leave the group. The last person left wins a beautifully decorated cake."

"Where are we going to get all the cakes?" asked Josh.

"That's the fun part," Miss Bingham said. "We're going to make them. After lunch, the school cooks are turning the kitchen over to us. We're going to bake and decorate twenty-one cakes. Twenty for the carnival and one for us."

Allison raised her hand. "How are we going to decorate the cakes?" she asked.

"Don't worry," said Miss Bingham. "I've made sure that we have lots of different colored frostings, sprinkles, and everything else we need to create some masterpieces."

"How about fake blood?" asked T.J. "I have a feeling that my cake might require some fake blood."

"You'll have to make do with red frosting," replied Miss Bingham.

Suddenly all of the students were cooking up fun ways to decorate cakes. Everyone but Spencer. He was busy thinking about tracking down a snake.

Chapter Seven

A Smelly Situation

At recess, Josh and Spencer went straight to the pile of leaves where they last saw Stretch.

"If you were a snake, where would you go?" asked Josh.

Spencer laughed. "If I were a snake, I would slither straight for the first girl I spotted. I would give her the biggest scare of her life."

"Me too," Josh said.

Just then they heard a bloodcurdling scream come from a group of second-grade girls. They were standing next to the monkey bars.

"Bingo!" said Spencer. "It sounds like Stretch is doing what snakes do best."

Spencer and Josh raced toward the screaming girls. By the time they got there, the girls had climbed onto the monkey bars and were pointing at some bushes.

"It went in there," shouted the girls.

Spencer marched straight to the biggest bush. Without even slowing down, he dropped to his knees and headed into the plant.

As he pushed past the branches, he could hear girls screaming, "Don't go in there! Are you crazy?"

Spencer smiled to himself and said, "Girls are such babies. They're scared to death of one little . . ." Spencer stopped.

"SKUNK!" he shouted. He backed up as fast as he could, but he wasn't fast enough. The skunk let out a blast that would have made King Kong faint.

Suddenly Spencer was the smelliest kid on the planet. Josh ran into the classroom shouting, "Miss Bingham, come quick. Spencer has been sprayed by a skunk. He's really stinking things up. Pretty soon there'll be people throwing up and fainting all over the place."

"Surely it can't be all that bad," said Miss Bingham.

At that instant, Spencer came staggering into the classroom. Miss Bingham's eyes started to water and she quickly plugged her nose.

Spencer was turning green. He had been in lots of smelly situations in the past, but nothing compared to this. "Miss Bingham, I have to go home. I don't feel so hot," he moaned.

"I think that's a good idea," gasped Miss Bingham. "In fact, the sooner you leave, the better."

Spencer was a walking stink factory. As he headed for the office, the hall cleared and doors slammed shut. Word of smelly Spencer traveled fast. By the time he got to the office, Mrs. Bradley, the school secretary, was hanging up the phone.

"Spencer, I just spoke to your mother," said Mrs. Bradley, holding a tissue over her mouth and nose. "She's at home and said that she would have a bath ready for you the instant you walked in the door."

Spencer marched out of the school and headed for home. When he walked in the front door he was met by his mother. "Head straight for the bathtub," said Mrs. Burton. "And you'd better use soap like you've never used soap before."

Spencer didn't ask any questions. He jumped in the bath and scrubbed so hard, he thought his skin was going to come off. When he got out of the tub, Spencer took another bath in his dad's cologne. He quickly got dressed and ran into the laundry room, where Mrs. Burton was folding clothes.

"How do I smell?" asked Spencer.

"You smell like you're ready to go on a date." Mrs. Burton laughed.

"I guess that's better than smelling like a skunk," said Spencer. "I'm going back to school. I've got to find Stretch."

"Stretch?" asked Mrs. Burton. "Who is Stretch?"

"Stretch is a sna — " Spencer stopped. He almost spilled the beans. "Stretch is a snazzy dresser. He's my new friend at school."

"What's his last name?" asked Mrs. Burton. "Maybe I know his parents."

"His last name is Snake," replied Spencer. "And believe me, you don't know Stretch's parents."

"That name doesn't ring a bell," said Mrs. Burton. "What does Mr. Snake look like?"

"Well . . ." Spencer hesitated. "He's real skinny and long — I mean tall. He has beady little eyes and sticks out his tongue a lot."

"That sounds like Ed Flake," said Mrs. Burton. "Are you sure Stretch's last name isn't Flake?"

"I'm sure," said Spencer. "I've got to go. It's Stretch's first day at school and he really needs me."

Chapter Eight

Snakoforous Snickertide

Miss Bingham was writing on the chalkboard when Spencer got back to class. She grinned when she spotted Spencer. "Are you smelling — I mean, feeling better?" she asked.

"It will take more than a little smelly skunk juice to get me down," replied Spencer.

"Good," said Miss Bingham. "We're going over some math problems."

Spencer grabbed his backpack and opened it. When he looked into the pack to find his math book, two beady little eyes were looking back at him. "Stretch!" yelled Spencer, forgetting that he was in the middle of class.

Miss Bingham turned around and asked, "Excuse me, what did you say?"

"Stretchachoo," said Spencer quickly. "I was just sneezing."

Spencer took out his math book and the snake. He put the book on his desk and held Stretch in his lap. He couldn't figure out how Stretch got into his pack.

When Spencer looked over at Josh, he found the answer. His best friend was giving him a big thumbs-up. While Spencer was home cleaning up, Josh had found Stretch and stuffed him in Spencer's pack.

"We're on page seventy-two," said Miss

Bingham. "Who knows the answer to problem three?"

Spencer read the math problem. It was a cinch. When he threw his hand into the air, Allison screamed. Spencer had accidentally raised the hand that was holding Stretch.

"Spencer, what on earth are you doing with that reptile in our class?" asked Miss Bingham.

Spencer's mind was whirling. A snake in class was against all the rules. He needed a whopper of an excuse this time.

Slowly he began, "Well, you see, Miss Bingham, this isn't an ordinary snake. This is a rare snake from the jungles of Argentina. It's a snakoforous snickertide."

"A snakoforous snickertide?" repeated Miss Bingham slowly.

"I know I should have asked before bringing him to class, but I really wanted everyone to see him before he goes back to Argentina," said Spencer.

T.J.'s hand shot into the air. Without waiting to be called on, he blurted out, "Can I hold the snakoforous snicker-tide?"

Suddenly the whole class was buzzing about Stretch. Calling the class back to attention, Miss Bingham said, "I can see that your minds are more on snakes than numbers. We have ten minutes before we need to go to the kitchen for our cake bake. We'll take that time for Spencer to tell us all about his unique snake."

The ten minutes zoomed by. Most of the boys and girls wanted to touch Stretch's soft skin.

"Okay, everybody," interrupted Miss Bingham. "It's time to put the snake away. We need to wash our hands and head for the kitchen. We have cakes to bake."

While everyone lined up at the sink, Josh whispered in Spencer's ear. "Nice job — you almost had *me* believing your crazy story. Where are you going to put Stretch while we make the cakes?"

"He has to come with us," answered Spencer. "We can't take the chance of losing him again."

"There's no way Miss Bingham would let us take him into the kitchen," said Josh.

"She'll never know," replied Spencer. "I have the perfect hiding place." Spencer tucked his shirt into his pants and then gently dropped Stretch down the front of his shirt.

The snake wiggled for a minute and then relaxed. After a rough day the inside of Spencer's shirt seemed like the perfect place to take a little nap.

"Can you tell I have a snake in my shirt?" asked Spencer.

"Snake? What snake?" replied Josh. Both boys laughed. They washed their hands and headed for the kitchen with the rest of the class.

Chapter Nine

Snake Baking

Everything in the kitchen was ready for the students when they arrived. All of the ingredients, bowls, and pans were lined up on the counter.

Miss Bingham quickly assigned every student a job. Spencer and Josh were put in charge of mixing the ingredients.

"Are we supposed to mix the stuff together with our hands?" asked Josh.

"Of course not," said Miss Bingham. "Use the wooden spoons."

"What wooden spoons?" asked Spencer.

"Now, what did I do with those spoons?" asked Miss Bingham. "Oh, now I remember. They're in the sack that's sitting on the cooler."

Spencer picked up the spoons and then opened the cooler. He licked his lips when he showed Josh the ice cream that was inside.

Forgetting to close the lid to the cooler, Josh and Spencer went to work stirring the ingredients together.

All of the commotion woke up Stretch. He was not the kind of snake to lay around when there was work to be done. Soon he was on the move. Spencer suddenly stopped stirring and started to laugh.

"What's so funny?" asked Josh.

"It's Stretch," replied Spencer. "He's tickling me." Spencer giggled and wiggled around.

All of a sudden the door to the kitchen opened and in marched the principal, Mr. Warner. All the kids but Spencer turned and gave Mr. Warner their full attention. Spencer was still laughing and doing the snake dance.

Miss Bingham walked over and stood next to Spencer. Spencer quickly came to attention. He bit his lip to keep from laughing.

Stretch stuck his head out the top of Spencer's shirt. He wanted to see what was going on. He looked at Miss Bingham and then stuck his little tongue out at Mr. Warner.

"I hope you're cooking up something good," said the principal.

Allison raised her hand and started to tell the principal all about the big cake bake.

While Allison talked, Stretch slipped out of Spencer's shirt. He slithered down Spencer's back and onto the counter.

Spencer started to breathe fast. He crossed his fingers, hoping that no one would spot the escaping snake. He planned on catching Stretch as soon as Mr. Warner left.

When Allison finished talking, Mr. Warner looked at Spencer and said, "Spencer, I need to see you in the office."

Spencer swallowed hard. "Mr. Warner, I really want to help with the cakes. Can I come later?"

"I'm afraid not," replied the principal.

While Spencer set down his spoon, he searched the counter quickly. There was no sign of Stretch. Then he noticed the

cake mixture. It seemed to be moving.

Oh, no! thought Spencer. Stretch is in the cake mix!

"Spencer," said Mr. Warner sternly, "we don't have all day."

Spencer slowly turned and followed his principal. He felt sick to his stomach. Miss Bingham's class was about to bake Big Jim McNalley's snake in a cake.

Chapter Ten

You're Under Arrest

Spencer had to walk fast to keep up with Mr. Warner. For some reason, the principal seemed to be in a hurry. "I have Sheriff Rowlan in my office," said Mr. Warner. "He wants to ask you a few questions."

Spencer couldn't believe his ears. The idea of talking to the sheriff made him forget all about Stretch swimming in cake batter.

When they entered the office, Sheriff Rowlan was talking on the phone. He looked very big and very official. Hanging up the phone, he stared right at Spencer.

"You probably know why I'm here," said the sheriff.

"I didn't do it," blurted out Spencer.

"Didn't do what?" Sheriff Rowlan asked.

"I didn't do whatever it is you have come to arrest me for," said Spencer.

The sheriff laughed. "I'm not going to arrest you. That skunk that sprayed you is still on the run. We don't want him to show up and spray anybody else. I thought you might have some helpful information about where he went."

Spencer lightened up. "You mean, you want to make me your deputy? Do I get a badge and a gun?"

"No," Sheriff Rowlan said with a

laugh. "But if we find the skunk, I'll give you a ride in my patrol car."

"All right!" shouted Spencer. "Come with me and I'll show you exactly where everything happened."

Outside, Spencer climbed into the bush where he had been sprayed. "Okay, pretend that I'm the skunk and you're me," said Spencer. "Stick your head in behind me."

The sheriff poked his head into the bush. Suddenly Spencer screamed at the top of his lungs. The sheriff reared up, hit his head on a branch, and fell out of the bush on his behind.

"What was that?" he yelled.

"That's when the skunk blasted me," said Spencer. "I wanted you to get the full effect. Of course, without the stinky part."

Then Spencer did his best skunk act

as he crawled over to a shrub. Sheriff Rowlan marched over to Spencer.

"He went right in there," whispered Spencer, pointing to an open space.

Sheriff Rowlan got down on his hands and knees and peered into the shrub. What he saw caused him to fall back on his behind for a second time. "It's in there!" he shouted.

All the commotion startled the skunk. The little animal let go of its big smell for a second time. In a matter of seconds, Sheriff Rowlan had been gassed.

The skunk came waddling out of the shrub like he wanted to escape from his own awful smell. "He's getting away," shouted Spencer, taking off after the stinky creature.

Sheriff Rowlan was in no shape to chase after anything. He just lay on the grass moaning.

Spencer followed the skunk down the sidewalk into the parking lot. The smelly little critter was desperately looking for a place to hide.

Spencer circled around in front of the skunk and opened the door of Sheriff Rowlan's car. He then snuck back behind the frightened animal and with great skill herded the skunk into the car.

"I've got you now," said Spencer, slamming shut the door of the car. "You're under arrest."

When Spencer got back to the shrub, Sheriff Rowlan was as green as the grass. "Where did that varmint go?" he asked.

"Don't worry," said Spencer. "I've got the suspect locked up."

"Good work," said the sheriff as he got to his feet. "I owe you a ride in the patrol car, but I think we should do it some other time."

Spencer saluted the sheriff and said, "Yes, sir. If you ever need help on any other smelly cases, just give me a call."

"You got it," said Sheriff Rowlan as he walked over and got into his patrol car. As he drove away, Spencer remembered that he'd forgotten to tell the sheriff where exactly he had locked up the skunk.

Suddenly the patrol car started weaving wildly back and forth. The flashing lights came on and the siren started to screech.

"I guess he found the skunk all by himself," said Spencer as he waved goodbye to Sheriff Rowlan.

Chapter Eleven

Eating Dynamite

Spencer was afraid to go back into the kitchen. How was he going to explain what Big Jim's snake was doing in a cake? He went in the rest room and hid in one of the stalls for over an hour. The entire time, he was trying to think of a plan.

Finally Spencer decided that every cake must be destroyed. That was the only way he could be sure no one would bite into a piece of cake and get a mouthful of snake.

Spencer snuck back to the kitchen and slowly opened the door. Everything was quiet. Miss Bingham had taken the students back to the classroom.

Walking into the room, Spencer spotted the cakes on the counter. They were all beautifully decorated. He picked up a broom and slowly walked toward them. Spencer lifted the broom and was about to whack the first cake when in walked his teacher.

"Spencer!" gasped Miss Bingham. "What are you doing?"

Spencer looked at Miss Bingham and then at the broom in his hand. "I just thought I would clean up a little," he said.

"We've already cleaned up," replied Miss Bingham. "Come along with me to class. We're about to eat cake and ice cream."

"CAKE!" screamed Spencer. "The cake we made today?"

"Yes," said Miss Bingham. "Why does that upset you? Are you allergic to cake?"

"Upset? Who's upset?" said Spencer. "I'm excited. I love cake!"

"Good," said Miss Bingham. "After your terrible experience with the skunk, I'm going to let you eat the first piece."

"Oh, boy," mumbled Spencer.

The whole class was buzzing when Miss Bingham and Spencer arrived. They could hardly wait to get a piece of cake and a scoop of ice cream.

Spencer closed his eyes while Miss Bingham sliced into the cake. She put a big piece on a plate and handed it to him. He put some cake on his fork and slowly put it in his mouth.

Spencer chewed liked he was eating dynamite. He knew that any second he would taste snake guts.

While T.J. got the ice cream out of the cooler, Miss Bingham handed the next piece of cake to Allison. Just as she was taking her first bite, Allison screamed, "It's that snake!"

Spencer spit the cake out of his mouth. Like a volcano erupting, chewed-up cake sprayed everywhere.

"I can explain," shouted Spencer. "I didn't mean for him to get baked in the cake, honest."

"What are you talking about?" asked Allison. "Your snake is in the cooler with the ice cream."

"Stretch!" yelled Spencer. "You jumped into the cooler instead of the cake mix. Good move, little buddy."

Spencer picked up his long friend and gave him a hug. Stretch was cold and a little sleepy but perfectly fine.

That night at the carnival, the cake-walk was a big hit. Miss Bingham wore a tall white chef's hat as she gave out the cakes to the winners.

Big Jim showed up with casts over both of his shoes. He spotted Spencer and Josh and hurried over. "I got so many signatures on my first cast, I put on another one," he said proudly.

Big Jim took out two dollars in change and handed the money to Spencer. "Here's your dough. Now where's my snake?"

"I've got him right here in my shirt," said Spencer. "He likes to sleep on my tummy."

Spencer took out Stretch and looked the snake right in the eye. "I'm going to miss you, little buddy," he said. Stretch stuck out his tongue and waved good-bye.

Spencer and Josh used their share of the money from Big Jim to buy tickets for the egg toss booth. They were going to settle the score from the egg war once and for all.

Spencer picked up an egg and aimed at Josh. "Bombs away!" he shouted. He was just letting go of the egg as Amber marched in front of him. Just as she opened her mouth to say, "I want my money," the egg crashed onto her favorite party blouse.

As the egg slime slid down Amber's shirt, Spencer raced over and put the dollar in her hand. "Try the cakewalk," he said. "It looks like your lucky night for food."

Amber started to scream, and Josh and Spencer started to run.

About the Author

Gary Hogg has always loved stories and has been creating them since he was a boy growing up in Idaho.

Gary is also a very popular storyteller. Each year he brings his humorous tales to life for thousands of people around the United States.

He lives in Huntsville, Utah, with his wife Sherry and their children, Jackson, Jonah, Annie, and Boone.

Here's a sneak peek
at the next

SPENCER'S adventures

#6 Let Go of That Toe!
by Gary Hogg

"Señor Spencer, what did you name your wonder dog?" asked Josh without even saying hello.

Spencer couldn't bring himself to tell Josh the sad news. "I haven't named him yet," he said.

"If he's fast, you could name him Lightning," suggested Josh.

"Well, he's not all *that* fast," said Spencer, as he looked at the turtle slowly creeping across the couch.

"Can I come over and see him do a few tricks?" asked Josh.

"Now isn't a good time," grumbled Spencer. "He's feeling a little sluggish."

"The whole class is counting on your new dog to be the star of the talent show," said Josh.

"Don't worry," replied Spencer. "I'll see you tomorrow." Spencer hung up the phone, grabbed his pet, and headed back to his room. Amber met him in the hall. When Spencer saw the way she was smiling, he knew there was going to be trouble.

"Get out of my way," ordered Spencer.

"Is your new dog feeling a little sluggish today?" asked Amber.

"You dirty rat," said Spencer. "You listened to my private phone conversation." He set his turtle down on the carpet and prepared for battle.

Amber turned to run, but Spencer grabbed her shirt. He had one arm wrapped around Amber's neck when she screamed, "My toe! My toe! It's trying to rip off my toe."

"What?" said Spencer, loosening his grip. Looking down, he saw his turtle had one of Amber's toes in its mouth. Amber shook her foot wildly, but the turtle would not turn her loose.

"He's trying to eat me!" yelled Amber.

"He can't eat you," shouted Spencer. "He doesn't have any teeth." Spencer reached down and pried his turtle off his sister's toe.

Amber's toe was perfectly fine, but that didn't stop her from grabbing her foot and hopping down the hall. "Spencer and his turtle are trying to kill me," she yelled as she bounced into the kitchen.

Spencer quickly grabbed his pet and headed out the front door. He'd only had his turtle for ten minutes and already he was in turtle trouble.

Getting into trouble is what Spencer does best

SPENCER'S
adventures
by Gary Hogg

Whenever Spencer falls into trouble, there's an adventure waiting to happen — the hairiest, scariest, sloppiest mess imaginable! Catch up with Spencer and all the laughs!

Look for these Spencer's Adventures:

❏ BCH93935-1 #1 Stop That Eyeball!
❏ BCH93936-X #2 Garbage Snooper Surprise
❏ BCH93937-8 #3 Hair in the Air
❏ BCH93938-6 #4 Toilet Paper Caper
❏ BCH93939-4 #5 Don't Bake That Snake!

$3.5
each!

Available wherever you buy books...or use this order form.
Scholastic Inc., P.O. Box 7502, Jefferson City, MO 65102

Please send me the books I have checked above. I am enclosing $_____ (please add $2.00 to cover shipping and handling). Send check or money order- no cash or C.O.D.s please.

Name_____Birthdate____/____/____

Address_____

City_____State/Zip_____

Please allow four to six weeks for delivery. Offer good in the U.S. only. Sorry, mail orders are not available to residents of Canada. Prices subject to change.

◣ SCHOLASTIC   SA49